Rascal

Linda Strachan
Illustrated by James Browne

Rigby

Josie took Rascal to see the vet.
Rascal didn't want to go.

ANIMAL HOSPITAL

Rascal didn't want to go in the door.
"Come on, Rascal," said Josie.

3

Rascal saw a cat.
Rascal liked cats.
He liked to chase them.
The cat saw Rascal.
She didn't like dogs.

Rascal wanted to play.
The cat didn't want to play.
She was scared.
"No, Rascal," said Josie.

Then Rascal saw a rabbit.
He liked rabbits.
He liked to chase them.
The rabbit saw Rascal.
He didn't like dogs.

Rascal wanted to play.
The rabbit didn't want to play.
He was scared.
"No, Rascal," said Josie.

Then the door opened
and a dog came in.
It was a **big** dog.
It was a **very big** dog.

Rascal saw the dog.
He didn't like big dogs.
They liked to chase him.

9

Rascal was scared.
He wanted to hide.
"No, Rascal!" said Josie.

The big dog looked at Rascal.
Rascal looked at the big dog.

"*Who's next?*" called the vet.
"Come on, Rascal!" said Josie.

Rascal didn't look at the cat.

Rascal didn't look at the rabbit.

Rascal didn't look at the big dog.

14

The big dog growled,
"**Grrr . . .**"
Rascal **RAN!**

Rascal ran to see the vet
as fast as he could.
"Good boy, Rascal!" said Josie.